THE INCREDIBLE WORM

Daniel Postgate

Albury Books

Into a brook
Dropped a worm
on a hook.

"Bless my soul!" said a trout
with a yell.
"What a marvelous treat
-Something tasty to eat.
And I'm just getting peckish
as well!"

The worm said, "I'm tasty
But don't be too hasty,
To eat me would be a great blunder...
As a matter of fact,
I can dance, sing and act.
**In a word – I'm an
        absolute wonder!"**

"So the worm entertains!
  Or at least so he claims...
  Well let us be the judge," said a pike.
  "We don't claim to be smart
  About theatre and art,
  But we certainly know what we like."

So the worm said, "Right-o!
Let's get on with the show!"
And he put on a tiny top hat.
And from somewhere there came
A small sparkling cane.
"It's a promising start," said a sprat.

Then the worm sang a song,
It was bold, it was strong,
And yet sentimental and sweet.
Asked a bass, "Is it wrong
To be moved by a song
From a creature I'd happily eat?"

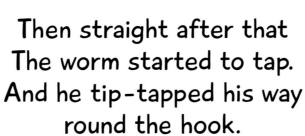

Then straight after that
The worm started to tap.
And he tip-tapped his way
round the hook.

All the fish found his dancing
And prancing entrancing -

Soon others came
over to look.

Then the worm played guitar;
He played Blues, Rock and Ska.
He played Funk, he played Punk,
 he played Jive.
All the fish folk applauded
And felt well-rewarded
For letting the worm stay alive.

Then the worm told
those folks
Such hilarious jokes
That they howled like
they hadn't for years.

"Oh, you've tickled me pink!"
Said a freshwater shrimp
As it laughed through
its saltwater tears.

The worm smiled and bowed,
And said thanks to the crowd.
"My dear friends, you're
   a generous bunch.
Now, I really must go—"
But the trout said, "Oh no.
You're talented, clever
And funny, however...

All the fish made a fuss,
They said, "What about us?"

"Don't be daft," said the trout,
"he's too small.
Come along, let's not quibble
He's my little nibble -
I spotted him first, after all!"

Then the worm whispered sweetly,
"Before you all eat me,
Please let me perform
                one last time...

"Gather close. **Take a look!**"
Then he climbed up the hook
And he tugged, very hard,
on the line.

With a sudden great swish
Something swung past the fish
And into a net they were bundled...

With a flip and a flop,
And a splash and a plop,
Straight into a churn
    they were tumbled!

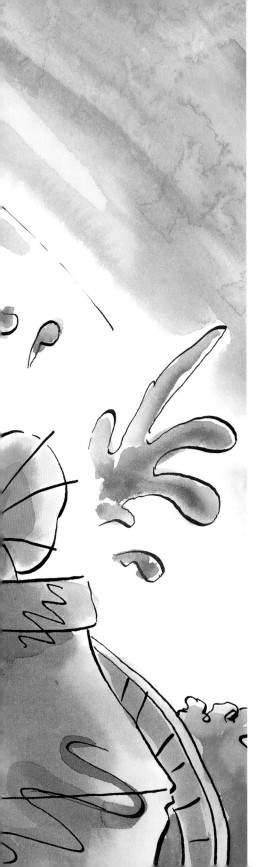

"So now what did you think
Of the show?" asked the shrimp.
Said the trout,
"Well, I really must say...

That young worm is a star.
Without doubt he'll go far...
At the end I was quite
swept away!"

The boy cried, "Hoorah!
That's my best catch by far!"
And he picked up his battered
   old churn.
With a splosh and a splish
He went off with his fish,

And of course,
His incredible worm!

For Poppy

This edition published in 2020
in association with Crane Press

First published in 2012
Albury Books, Albury Court,
Albury, Thame, Oxfordshire, OX9 2LP

www.AlburyBooks.com

Text & illustrations © Daniel Postgate 2012

ISBN: 978-1-910571-20-0